Disney · PIXAR

Look and Find®

INCREDIBLES 2

we make books come alive™

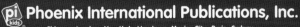

pi kids® **Phoenix International Publications, Inc.**

Chicago · London · New York · Hamburg · Mexico City · Paris · Sydney

Meet Bob Parr. Bob used to fight crime as Mr. Incredible, but now Bob keeps his supersuit in the closet. These days he focuses on being a Super dad instead. Super dads know breakfast is the most important meal of the day, so Bob is making French toast for his family. Yum!

While the family gathers around the kitchen counter, help Bob locate these items they can't leave home without:

Violet's backpack

stack of Violet's textbooks

Helen's mask

Helen's supersuit

Dash's math homework

Dash's backpack

After breakfast, Bob makes sure Violet and Dash are ready for school. He hands them their things and guides them out the door. Super mom Helen needs to head out, too. She'll be fighting crime while Bob handles things at home. Looks like everyone will be on time. Nice job, Bob!

But Bob still worries—he knows firsthand it's a tough world out there. Help everyone reach their destinations safely by pointing out these obstacles:

these bullies

peashooter

suspicious character

spy camera

paper airplane

falling girder

Now that it's just Bob and Jack-Jack, it's time to get the house cleaned up. Bob wants to start with the Great Room, where there are lots of boxes he is eager to unpack.

Before Bob can start sifting through his own stuff, he needs to clear a path! Help him find these baby things:

baby book

bottle

bib

rattle

diapers

pacifier

Bob is busy making lunch when Helen calls to check in. She is having a stressful day. Bob assures her everything is going smoothly and that there's nothing at home to worry about. She should feel free to give one hundred percent of her attention to work.

While Helen's on the phone, give her a hand by pointing out these villains:

Bob would love some alone time, so he tries to convince Edna Mode to watch Jack-Jack for a little while. It is hard enough to get Edna to keep an eye on one Jack-Jack, but then Jack-Jack starts to multiply!

While Bob and Edna struggle to get a handle on the situation, look for these Jack-Jacks:

Violet and Dash make it home safely from school, and they are hungry! Bob tries to get TV dinners done fast enough to distract the Super siblings.

Before Dash dashes away and Violet vanishes, help secure this fragile stuff:

Superlative
Super award

flower vase

family photo

#1 Dad mug

lamp

fancy statuette

After dinner, Bob sits for a minute to catch his breath—uh-oh, looks like he's nodding off. In the time it takes Bob's eyelids to droop, Jack-Jack toddles through the kitchen door, and now he's chasing a raccoon bandit around the side yard!

Jack-Jack and the raccoon are making a mess! While Bob gets Jack-Jack back inside, help tidy up the yard by spotting this trash:

battered box

squished tissue

crushed can

discarded drumstick

crumpled carton

squandered slices

It's almost bedtime, but Bob hasn't seen a Super power yet that's strong enough to make his kids pick up after themselves. He is just about to nag them—and then he nods off again. When Helen gets home from her assignment, she lets him sleep. She knows fighting grime is just as hard as fighting crime. Bob really *is* a Super dad!

Give the Parrs one more helping hand by spotting this scattered stuff:

Jack-Jack's
teething toy

Violet's hairband

Helen's purse

Dash's shoe

Dash's
action figures

Violet's jacket

Violet and Dash like it when Bob makes French toast for breakfast. Head back to the kitchen and find these ingredients he needs:

IncrediButter

milk, 2% Super

Super eggs

simply incredible vanilla extract

thumb-crushed nutmeg

hand-ground cinnamon

Supers are in the spotlight! Retrace the Parrs' paths to school and work, and spot these conversation starters:

Bob can't be blamed for wanting to relive his glory days. Visit the Great Room again and find these old news clippings he keeps stashed away:

Elastigirl's exploits are attracting some attention! Return to her battle with the baddies and spot these news choppers following the action:

Edna Mode's time with Jack-Jack has convinced her to stick to fashion design. Revisit her lab and find these sensational sketches:

Dart back to the dining room and gather up Dash's scattered homework:

Jack-Jack and the raccoon leave quite a mess behind them. Go back to the yard and help Bob find these things they knocked over:

upside-down umbrella   broken basketball hoop   seat not at the table   table tossed   gnome in the bush   spilt grill

A Super family needs to be prepared for anything. Sneak back to the living room and locate six secret exits marked by this logo: